Table of Contents

Dedication

Every day we make choices...
to be powerful or weak
to love or close ourselves off
to be brave or fearful
to be happy or sad
to be honest or lie to ourselves
Believe in yourself!
You are special, beautiful, smart,
strong and worthy.
Let your light shine on the world...
Don't shrink into insignificance.
The choice is yours.
Katrina x

Julia Jones is a typical teenage girl. She wants to fit in, have friends, be loved and happy. As you follow her journey, think about the choices she is making. Think about how you would act in the same situations and challenges.

Frightened...

I stared in horror at what confronted me. The likeness was uncanny. It had the same long, brown hair and hazel eyes as my own, but the ghoulish grin was hideous. Numb with shock, I stood there, my mind reeling with confusion and panic. It took every last reserve of self-control, to contain the frightened screams that I felt bubbling inside. My mouth agape, I could not take my eyes from the ugly figure that had been shoved into the back of my locker.

It was a child's toy, a remnant from a long forgotten doll collection, but it had been remodeled to resemble me. A scattering of light freckles had been dotted across the nose and cheeks, probably with a permanent marker. In addition, a dirty brown stain had been drawn on the side of one leg and I glanced down at the birthmark that covered the inside of my own thigh, the mark I'd been tormented about from a young age.

That hideous smile, the evil smirk that was painted on, made my skin crawl. But the most disturbing and horrific detail was the fact that there were three long, thick sewing needles protruding grotesquely from the torso and two more had been thrust brutally into each side of the head.

With a gasp of realization, the words 'voodoo doll,' entered my mind. I had read somewhere that African tribes had once used this type of witchcraft to cast spells on village members. In many cases, the victims became violently ill, and sometimes the effect was so intense that people actually died.

Then, without warning, everything went black.

One month earlier...

This couldn't be happening! This sort of thing happened to other people, not me!

White faced, I stared at my dad.

"Are you for real?" I thought to myself. "One week before Christmas and you drop this bombshell on our family!"

Speechless, I glared at him, my eyes turning dark with anger. My mother used to tease me about the color of my eyes when I was younger. "Black-eyed Suzie," she used to call me. According to her, that was the color my eyes turned whenever I was angry. But I hated her taunting. I hated that expression and it just made me angrier to hear her using it. That would only encourage her to tease me further. I used to really hate my mother for that!

But now it was my dad who had to bear the brunt of my evil look.

Seriously, how could he do this to us?

Without a word, I ran to the sanctuary of my bedroom and slammed the door shut. Throwing myself down on the bed, I grabbed hold of the tattered and worn teddy bear that still sat forlornly propped up on my pillow, the one remaining stuffed toy that I would always keep. And I broke down into a heart-wrenching sob.

My world as I knew it was ending. It was a nightmare I wanted to wake up from and never experience again. But I knew that was impossible.

At that moment, I just wanted to disappear.

Changes...

As I lay there, my pillow drenched with tears, I stared longingly out the window. My mom had tried comforting me, but I just wanted to be left alone. Nothing she could say would help.

It just wasn't fair! Surely there was another solution. I knew that my parents had money problems, especially after Dad lost his job. I'd overheard them whispering several times during the past few weeks, and then they'd cast guilty glances my way as soon as they realized I was within earshot.

"What's going on?" I'd asked, curiously.

But my mother's reply was always the same. "Oh, nothing darling. Nothing for you to worry about!"

I can't believe they'd kept it from me. And then right before Christmas, Dad decided to break the news.

"We have to move back to the city. I start my new job in two weeks' time."

My life as I'd come to know it, would not exist anymore. It was bad enough that I'd had to sell my beautiful pony.

"We just can't afford to keep her here any longer," Dad had tried to explain.

That was three months ago and I was still aching with misery at the loss of my beloved friend. That's what she had become, the one constant figure of trust in my life. The one on whose friendship and loyalty I could always rely. And then, in the blink of an eye, she'd been whisked away.

The memory of the horse trailer driving down our driveway and out through the old wooden gate, would haunt me forever. And in my dreams, I could still hear her whinny, her morning call when I would rush out to the stables to greet her. Her warm breath nuzzled my hand as she looked for the regular treats that I always had ready. She had been the light of my life but just like a candle in the wind, that light had been extinguished with one quick puff and was now gone forever.

A sudden cold draught burst through my open window and I jumped out of bed to close it. The temperature had been unseasonably warm for that time of year, and I had opened my window earlier in the day to welcome the rays of sunshine that danced on the patterned rug beside my bed.

As I stared out onto the grassy fields of our twenty hectare property, my heart filled with sadness. There would be no more horse riding, no more hanging out in the stables with friends and no more living in what I had come to call my home.

We had moved there, three years earlier, leaving behind our family home which was situated in the township of another state, over a thousand miles away. It could have been on another planet, the distance was so great. Once again, it was Dad's job that had forced us to be uprooted from everything that was familiar. I recalled the vivid memory of being told I had to be separated from everything I knew and loved; my home, my school, my friends. And it was my two best friends, Millie and Blake, who I had found it hardest to say goodbye to. I remembered how distraught I had been at the thought of not being able to see them each day. Millie was my closest friend ever and Blake... he was my one true love.

That was how I had felt back then. But with the passing of time, our friendship had gradually been reduced to an occasional phone call at Christmas and birthdays. It was then that I realized Millie's birthday had just recently passed by and I had completely forgotten about it.

Glancing towards the myriad of photo frames that adorned my bookcase, I spotted photos of Millie and I, so happy and totally inseparable; BFFs was what we had once called ourselves. Then another image caught my eye. I reached for the photo that sat towards the back of the shelf, the one that was covered in dust. His handsome face stared back at me. The beautiful warm smile that had once made my heart melt, still managed to create a small, familiar flutter in the pit of my stomach.

I remembered the devastation I had felt at being separated from the boy I loved. He was my soul mate, the one to whom I could tell anything, even my deepest darkest secrets. We'd promised that the distance would not keep us apart, but over time, life had just seemed to get in the way. And according to Millie when we last spoke, Blake had started going out with someone else.

To return to that old life was not something I had ever expected to happen and I knew that it could never be the same.

A gut wrenching fear abruptly took hold and I shivered with apprehension about what lay ahead.

"I'm not moving!" I screamed loudly. "You can't make me move again!"

With frustration and anger, I thrust the photo frame I was holding at the closed door, the glass shattering into pieces all over the floor. Through tear filled eyes, I glared angrily down at the image of Blake's smiling face, staring happily back up at me.

Then, feeling totally distraught and completely overwhelmed, I burst into uncontrollable wracking sobs.

The return...

When our car pulled up at the driveway of our old house,
the one from my past life, I stared from the window in
disbelief. The sick feeling that had wormed its way into the
depths of my being felt ready to erupt. I had hardly spoken a
word over the past weeks. My mother's anxious looks,
followed by her desperate attempts to console me had been
of no use.

Miraculously, Dad had found a buyer for our country
property almost straight away, and we'd had to pack and
move as quickly as possible. I hadn't even had a chance to
return to school after the Christmas break to say goodbye to
everyone, and it was only my closest friends who I'd
bothered to call.

It was all just too heart breaking to even think about right
now but what was annoying me most was my brother's
whole attitude towards the crisis. I'd thought he would be
even more upset than me, but surprisingly, he had managed
to handle it all really well.

"I don't mind going back," was his response when he heard
the news. "It's too boring out here in the country, anyway.
And besides," he'd added with a grin, "there are so many
more hot girls at my old school!"

Girls! I swear that's all he thinks about these days. It's
actually a miracle that he even manages to get any
schoolwork done. And moving in the middle of his final
senior year obviously is the worst scenario ever. But he
doesn't seem to care and it really annoyed me not to have his
support. Out of everyone in the family, I seemed to be the
only one who didn't want the change.

"She'll be okay!" I had heard my dad say to Mom the other night. "Just give her some time, she'll adjust."

Well if he thought I was going to be happy about the situation, he had that totally wrong! He had no idea what it was like for someone my age. Having to sell our farm and return to our old home in Carindale was all so humiliating. What was everyone going to say? What were they going to think? And apart from that, I was not looking forward to going to a new school.

Mom had tried to convince me that it would all be great. "The new high school that's been built while we were away looks amazing. And as well, Julia, we're so lucky to be able to move back into our old house! You'll have your bedroom back again and we can do it up just the way you always wanted."

I guess I should be grateful that my parents had decided to keep our house when we moved. A family from out of town had been renting it the whole time, but had recently bought their own place so it was available for us to move back into. At least that was something in our favor.

I followed my parents inside and trudged up the old familiar staircase to my bedroom. Situated at the end of the hallway was the panelled green door that led to my private place, and I raced towards it, desperate to have some time on my own.

Bursting through the door, I was hit with the nostalgia of my childhood. The teddy bear wallpaper still decorated the walls and my old pink curtains hung loosely from the window frame. I remembered choosing the fabric. The little white flowers surrounded by a pretty pink background had been my favorite and I was so proud of the outcome when they were finally fitted to the window.

Recollections of the endless amount of time I had spent staring out onto the garden below came to mind and precious memories flooded my thoughts. It was as if the past three years were totally surreal and hadn't even happened. Visions of Millie and Blake and the times we had shared filled my awareness and I wondered what their lives were like now.

So many times, I had considered calling them or trying to keep regular contact but I always seemed to have more important things to do. It had been so long since we'd last spoken. Surely though, they'd be happy to see me and have me back? We used to be so close. Perhaps my mom was right and everything would all just fall into place. I felt a spark of hope lift my spirits ever so slightly and then, a vision of Blake, his arms wrapped around my shoulders as he hugged me close, crept into my mind.

Maybe, just maybe, things could return to how they were. I felt my lips twitch, a small smile forming at the corners of my mouth. And then I remembered that Millie had said Blake was going out with someone else.

Three years had passed by after all, so what could I expect? Not that I had found another boy to replace Blake during that time. As I turned to face the open door, something caught my eye. It was a blue scrawl on the wall next to where my bed used to be positioned. The tiny heart I had drawn, all those years ago still remained in clear view. And the letters inside reminded me once more of the romance we had once shared... *JJ Loves BJ*

Julia Jones Loves Blake Jansen...would I ever find another boy as special? Somehow I felt that did not seem possible!

Doubts...

I decided to give Millie a call.

"Hi, Millie!" I imagined the words I would say. "It's Julia – you remember me...your long lost friend? Well, guess what! I'm back!"

"OMG, Julia!!! This is the best news I've ever heard!!" I pictured her smiling face in my mind, the face that I remembered so well and the reaction that I so desperately needed to hear.

Picking up the phone, I keyed in her number. It was amazing how clearly I remembered it, even though I hadn't called her for so long. I was sure that her number would forever be ingrained in my memory. Almost every evening after dinner, we would call each other, sometimes talking for an hour or more.

"How can you have so much to say?" my mother would ask. "You've been at school together all day and you still manage to spend so long on the phone! Hang up now and go and do your homework!"

That same scenario was repeated almost every night. I'd nod in agreement to my mom, but keep on talking until thirty more minutes had passed by and she was threatening to rip the phone out of my hand.

Impatiently, I waited for the line to connect. Busy signal. Great!

I hung up and waited a few moments before trying again.

"Hello, is this Mrs. Spencer?"

"No, I'm sorry, she's not here" was the reply.

"I was actually wanting to speak to Millie," I continued.

"Oh, I'm sorry, dear," the high pitched tone announced through the earpiece. "You won't be able to speak to her today. Actually you'll be waiting quite a while. They've gone traveling around Europe for a few months, the lucky things. Haven't you heard? I was sure that Millie had told all her close friends."

The annoying voice prattled on and on, as I stood there silently; my mind reeling in disbelief.

"Hello? Hello? Are you there?" continued the screechy voice. "Can I take a message for you?"

"Ah, no, it's ok. Thank you!" I replied and quickly hung up.

Sinking to the floor, I shook my head in total dismay. School was starting in two days' time and Millie would not be there. And the fact of the matter was that she was going to be away for quite some time. She had gone to Europe with her family and I'd been completely unaware of it. I felt so guilty.

But perhaps if I'd been allowed to have a Facebook account, or even Instagram, I would know what had been going on in her life.

That was never going to happen while my mother was around though. She was so strict and old fashioned, a real control freak. "You don't need that sort of distraction," she always said. "And besides, I've heard too many stories of cyber-bullying and terrible things going on all because of social media. You don't need it, Julia. Just pick up the phone to stay in contact with your friends. That is all that's necessary!"

Well what did my mother know! If I was allowed to be like any other normal teenager, it would be so simple to stay in contact with everyone.

The familiar uneasy feeling began to form once more in the pit of my stomach, the recurring one that I was experiencing a lot of lately.

"Back with your oldest, dearest friends," Mom had said to me just that morning, in the sickening, reassuring tone she was always using. "I'm sure Millie is going to be so excited to see you again!"

"Yeah, right!"

Taking a deep breath I picked up the phone and tried Blake's number.

I could feel my palms sweating and held my breath as I listened to the dull sound of the dial tone.

"What if he's not home?" I thought to myself. "What if he's gone away as well? And worse still, what if he answers and doesn't want to talk to me?"

The phone seemed to ring forever.

"Pick up! Pick up!" I said into the receiver.

Then just as I was about to put the phone down, a deep male voice answered.

"Hello?"

"It must be his dad. It sounds just like his dad. I think I'll just hang up." The thoughts raced frantically through my mind but I could not bring myself to speak.

"Hello," the voice repeated. "Is anyone there?"

"H…Hello," I stammered, my voice croaky with nerves. "Can I please speak to Blake?"

"This is Blake," was the unexpected reply.

"Blake?" I questioned. "You sound so different!"

"Julia! Julia, is that you?" His voice had become more familiar, definitely deeper than when we'd last spoken, but certainly familiar.

I stood there silently, feeling foolish, but I just couldn't bring myself to speak.

"Julia, that *is* you, isn't it? I'd know that voice anywhere!"

"Yes, Blake. It's me."

"This is incredible," he laughed. "I haven't heard from you in so long!"

"I know. I'm sorry. I've been really slack." I sat down on my bed and stared blankly at my reflection in the mirror. I felt so awkward and had no idea what to say.

"How are you? And what have you been up to?" his friendly tone was reminiscent of the same Blake I once knew; the Blake from my past life before everything had changed.

"We moved back into our old house a few days ago." I explained. "Dad has a new job here so we had to sell the farm and come back."

I held my breath and waited anxiously for his response.

"Wow! Now I'm really in shock!" Was it my imagination or had his enthusiasm dropped somewhat.

Silence came between us then, an awkward silence that I had never experienced when talking with Blake before.

"So you'll be going to school here as well?"

"Yeah," I replied.

There seemed to be a moment's hesitation and then the half-hearted response. "That's so cool!"

"So I guess I'll see you on Monday?" My heart was hammering in my chest and a flood of nausea churned in my stomach.

"Yeah, worse luck. It's so bad that the holidays are over." Then almost as an afterthought, he added, "But it'll be great to see you, Julia!"

"Yeah, you too, Blake; it's been so long! Anyway, I just rang to say hello. I'll see you on Monday."

"Ok, see you on Monday, Julia," and with a click of the phone he was gone.

I brushed the tears from my cheeks. They'd begun falling and I was helpless to stop them. I looked into the mirror once more.

"You're pathetic," I said to myself. "What did you expect; that he'd be throwing himself at you, after being apart for three years?"

Well that obviously wasn't going to happen.

I desperately tried to swallow my disappointment. The situation totally sucked. "Maybe I can just run away from home," I thought fleetingly.

But where would I go? I had hardly any money in the bank and I'd probably end up as one of those street kids you hear about, doing drugs and in a total mess.

I could hear my mother calling me to go downstairs for dinner. I wished I could ignore her and just go to sleep and never wake up. But I couldn't stand the thought of her coming into my room and telling me that everything was going to be okay.

With a deep sigh of resignation, I stood up and went downstairs; not that I had any appetite. Right then, the thought of food just made me feel ill. Two more days; two more days of freedom and then my life was going to change yet again. A new school, new friends – or so I hoped!

Right then, I did not feel at all positive about my future, but if I had only known what was in store, perhaps I would have chosen the option of running away after all!

First day back...

As I entered the gates, it was as though a thousand pairs of eyes were staring in my direction. I felt like an object on show at some type of event, where people had to check out the quality of the merchandise.

Keeping my eyes focused on the footpath in front of me, I gripped my books closely to my chest and made my way towards the office entrance. Thankfully, over the course of the weekend, I'd managed to contact a couple of old friends who were actually pleased to hear I was back and as prearranged, they were waiting by the glass doors that led to the office.

"At least I'm not going to be a total loner. That would have really sucked!" The thoughts racing through my head were a mixture of relief and anxiety but the warm welcome from my friends and their genuine pleasure at seeing me again was exactly what I needed to put me at ease.

After exchanging quick hugs, they directed me to the administration desk where I was able to sort out my timetable. To my enormous relief, it appeared that we shared some classes, although I had been assigned to a completely different English class to each of them and typically, that was the first class I had to attend.

We agreed to meet back at the same spot for morning recess and I then headed in the direction of the lockers. As I shoved my books into the locker that would be mine for the semester, I was aware that the area was bustling with students who were taking the opportunity to catch up on all the holiday gossip before being ushered into their first class.

Then, just as I pushed the door of my locker closed, the sound of a familiar voice made my head turn.

"Julia Jones!"

Spinning around I found myself face to face with Sara Hamilton. And in the blink of an eye, I was engulfed in the memories of my past.

The nightmares from middle school struck me with the sheer force of a sledgehammer. Being locked in a tiny tin shed that was hidden away in the depths of rugged bushland was a vision I would rather forget. My screams of terror as the claustrophobia kicked in, were clear in my mind and I could feel the fear that had ripped through me, as clearly as if it had happened only yesterday.

That was only one of many vivid and frightening moments that I had tried to wipe from my memory banks, and time and distance had helped to make that possible. But the sight of Sara, the person who had caused me so much grief for so long, triggered those long forgotten and unwanted memories to reappear. Although we had parted as so-called friends, I knew that I would never really forgive her intense bullying and hatred, all those years ago.

She stood there with her eyebrows raised questioningly and her old, self-assured confident stance. Looking directly at her, I could not help but notice that she was still as pretty as ever. Time hadn't changed that, and if anything, she was probably even more beautiful than when I had last seen her.

Her long, blonde hair was cut in the latest style. It was parted in the middle and hung loosely in gorgeous layers down the length of her back. The olive complexion, that I had always envied, glowed with a golden tan that set off her striking blue eyes as she stared intensely back at me.

How on earth could she have such a stunning tan in the middle of winter? Maybe it's a spray on, or I wouldn't be surprised if she's been away to some tropical paradise during the Christmas break! The thoughts raced through my mind as I stood there staring in disbelief.

"Sara!" I exclaimed, as I desperately tried to hide the shock waves passing through my body. "I didn't expect to see you here. I'd heard that you and your family had moved away."

"Yeah we did. But my dad was transferred back here at the beginning of last semester, so here I am! And what about you? What brings you back?"

"My dad is working here again as well, so we moved back a week ago."

"Oh, wow! So we're all here together again, just like the old days!" There was no mistaking the sarcasm in her voice and I felt my skin crawl.

This couldn't be happening, it just couldn't. Surely, I was going to wake up any minute and sigh with desperate relief that it had been one really bad dream, over and done with, never to occur again.

I walked with her towards the classroom that I had located on the map I was given by the office staff. All the while, Sara prattled on as if nothing whatsoever was wrong. But I knew her too well and although she had made amends all those years ago, I knew that deep down she would never change. People like her always wanted to be in control. They had that deep-seated need to make themselves look and feel better than others.

I never could figure out why Sara was like that. She was the best looking girl in our grade, she had a heap of loyal girlfriends, boys seemed to fall at her feet, and as well as that, her family was so wealthy that she had everything money could buy.

Her excuse had been that she was jealous of me! Hmph! Jealous of me…how pathetic is that! How could someone like Sara possibly be jealous of me?

Then as if things could not get any worse, she walked into the same classroom that I was headed for.

"Nooooo!" I screamed in my mind. "Please tell me she's not in my English class!"

And as if in response to my unspoken statement, she turned and smiled sweetly, "Looks as though we're in the same class. It really will be just like the old days!"

Then with a flick of her long hair, she disappeared to the back of the room. But it was what happened next that shocked me more than ever!

Already sitting in the back row, with one vacant seat next to him which was obviously reserved for a friend, was the most gorgeous looking guy I think I had ever seen in my entire life.

He was deep in conversation with the person sitting on the other side and was oblivious to the fact that I was standing at the doorway, gawking at him. I simply could not help myself. It was as though my feet were rooted to the spot.

He flicked back the long, brown locks of hair that hung untidily over his eyes and I watched his face light up in response to some humorous comment or joke made by his friend. That beautiful smile caused my heart to throb and I looked on adoringly from my spot at the front of the room.

Forcing myself to take the nearest seat, I glanced discreetly in his direction. It was then that his face turned, but not towards mine. That beautiful smile that I had just been drooling over, burst into a wide grin as he wrapped his arms in a tight embrace around the girl who had just greeted him.

As she sat down in the seat he had saved for her, Sara looked towards the front of the room, her eyes piercing into mine. Totally smug, she turned to face him once more and planted a possessive kiss on his smiling lips. With her arm around him, she glanced at me again and it was then that he and I made eye contact.

Looking slightly pale and as if the color had drained from his face, he stared at me, his eyes riveted to mine.

The realization shook me to my very core. The love of my life, Blake Jansen was going out with Sara Hamilton! Finally, after years of torment and shameless flirting, she had managed to succeed in winning him over.

And as I turned slowly towards the front of the class, I could feel her evil stare burning into my back.

My head was spinning, my mind reeling with disbelief. I had to fight to keep down the nausea that was rising to my throat and it took every last reserve of self-control to stay in my seat. All I wanted to do was run out of the room. Run away forever!

When the teacher introduced me to the class, I was barely able to nod in acknowledgement. Turning bright red in embarrassment at being singled out, I put my head down and tried to focus on the book in front of me. But my eyes filled with tears, the words turned to a blur and the teacher's voice became a droning background monotone.

Screaming inside, I gritted my teeth and checked the clock on the wall at what seemed like thirty second intervals, willing the hands to move so that the class would end and I could make my escape.

"Breathe, Julia! Just breathe!" The words flashed through my mind and I gulped down the oxygen I'd been depriving myself of, until finally, the bell went and everyone was allowed to file out for morning recess.

I could not get out the door and down the corridor quickly enough. Bursting into the fresh air, I made my way across the square of grass at the front of the school and found a spot under a tall, leafy tree where I'd be hidden from view. I knew that I'd arranged to meet my friends but I just couldn't bear to face anyone right then. I just needed to be alone.

It all made sense now. Blake's odd reaction to my phone call the other day was no longer a mystery.

"What's his problem?" I'd thought to myself after talking to him. "Even if he does have a girlfriend, surely he would still be happy to see me!"

At the time, I could not figure it out, but now it had become perfectly clear. Blake was completely aware of the trouble I'd experienced with Sara for so long. The bullying and mean, taunting behavior had gone on and on and on. Until eventually, I stood up to her and she decided to leave me alone. But she'd always been in love with Blake. I knew that beyond any doubt. She could have had any guy in the school, but the only one she really wanted was Blake.

Now, finally, he was hers. Well she could have him, I decided! If that was the type of person he wanted to be with then they deserved each other! With a huge sigh, I stood up and made my way back to the classrooms. The bell had gone and I didn't want to make a spectacle of myself by being late for my next class.

With my head down and avoiding eye contact with anyone, I went to my locker to retrieve my Math book. I could feel the eyes of onlookers as I walked past and I overheard one girl who was wearing a tight fitting, low cut top that I thought was totally inappropriate for school, say to her friend, "That's the new girl! Apparently she used to go out with Blake Jansen."

"No way!" replied her friend, looking me up and down, obviously being critical of the blue jeans and faded t-shirt that I was wearing.

"Is it so surprising that Blake actually went out with me?" I thought, giving her a hard look and continuing on down the corridor. But all the while, I could hear the sound of their laughter, ringing in my ears.

The remainder of the day was uneventful for which I was extremely grateful. I just couldn't have dealt with any more surprises. Although I had double classes for every subject, which was not a pleasant way to start the semester, I was really pleased to find that neither Blake nor Sara were in any of them. During lunch break I was able to catch up with my friends and apologize for not meeting up with them earlier. Having some friendly faces to hang out with …was the biggest relief of all. Otherwise, I was sure I'd be spending lunch break sitting all on my own.

At the sound of the final bell later in the afternoon, I made my way to the bus stop and just managed to hop on the bus before it pulled out from the kerb. That would have been all I needed, to miss the bus and have to walk home. When I climbed aboard and reached the top of the steps, I looked down the aisle to see that every seat was taken. Except for one at the very front next to a nerdy looking boy covered in pimples. Rolling my eyes skyward, I sat down next to him and stared out the window lost in thought.

Visions of my school in the country and all my friends there, flashed through my mind. I could easily picture them, laughing and joking with each other, and making plans to hang out over the coming weekend. In my head, I could see all their faces, beaming with the joy of just being together. That vision should have included me. I should have been a part of it, not stuck here in misery! It just wasn't fair!

Then I thought of our farm and my beloved pony, Bella. I wondered what she was doing right then. Was she happy? And were her new owners looking after her? I had given them a list of her favorite treats and the brands of horse feed that she preferred. I missed her so much and I wondered if she missed me.

My eyes began to well with tears and I was grateful that the bus had reached my stop so that I could get off before anyone noticed I was crying. I stood sadly on the footpath waiting for the bus to pass by so I could cross over the road. Then, quite unexpectedly, I caught the eye of a boy seated next to the window towards the back. He had been lost in thought himself, when he abruptly realized I was standing there. Then his head whipped towards me in recognition.

I don't know who was more surprised that we had been on the same bus, Blake or me. But all I could do was stare heart-broken back at him as the bus pulled away and disappeared down the street.

Something is not right...

As I walked through the open front door of our house, I was
hit with the sound of a strange voice coming from the top
floor. This was followed by uncharacteristic fits of laughter
from my mother. I definitely wanted to avoid having to talk
to Mom and some stranger, so I attempted to sneak quietly
up the stairs to the solitude and safety of my bedroom. But
as I got to the top stair, I found it was actually my room that
the voices were coming from.

Staring at the scene in front of me, I looked from my mom to
the stranger. He was hammering away at my window frame
while she sat comfortably on my bed deep in conversation,
all the while laughing easily at some joke that they had
obviously been sharing.

I immediately noticed something different about my mom.
The relaxed and cheerful expression on her face was almost
foreign to me; it had been so long since I had seen her
looking that way. Reluctant to announce my presence, I
hesitated, unsure of whether I should interrupt. But at the
same time I was overcome with a seething annoyance at the
invasion of my privacy. This was my room and how dare
they invade my space! I just wanted to yell, "Get Out!!"

But forcing the words to remain unspoken, I stood there
transfixed at the scene in front of me.

It was the man who noticed me first and for some reason, I
took an instant dislike to him. This was not a common
occurrence as I was usually able to get along with most
people and had decided long ago, never to judge a book by
its cover. In this instance though, I wasn't sure whether to
call it intuition or gut instinct. Perhaps they're the same
thing, but whatever it was, I felt uneasy.

Looking up in surprise at my sudden appearance in the doorway, Mom, who was smiling happily and as if absolutely nothing at all was amiss, said with a grin, "Julia! Come and meet Barry! He's been here for the last couple of hours doing all the odd jobs around the place that desperately needed to be done. And you'll be so happy to know that your window has finally been repaired. You'll no longer have to prop it up with a book to keep it open!"

Looking at me expectantly, I could see her own smile fade somewhat when she realized the expression on my face did not display the gratification she had been anticipating.

Frowning, she opened her mouth to speak once more, but in order to avoid a confrontation, I quickly mumbled an insincere thanks, then turned around and headed back down the stairs to the kitchen.

I could clearly hear her words behind me. "I'm so sorry, Barry! She's normally not so rude. I think she's still coming to terms with having to move."

And it was his reply that irked me the most, "Oh, teenagers, Marian! I know how much trouble they can be!"

Incredulously, I shook my head. How dare they talk about me behind my back, and as I heard them laughing at my expense, I could feel my anger bubbling to the surface.

My father had left just that morning and would be away for the entire week. It appeared that his new job required him to travel regularly but right then, I wished that he was at home.

Seeing my mother sitting up there, completely comfortable and on a first name basis with some stranger who she had only just met, didn't seem right, and after slamming closed the fridge door in disgust at the sight of nothing to eat, I slumped down on the living room sofa.

Miserable! That was the only word I could find to describe how I felt. And I thought once more of the friends I had left behind in the country, the place I had come to call home. I knew I should give my best friend, Cassie, a call. We had promised to phone each other regularly, but my last conversation with her had left me sadder than ever.

She'd been so excited to go back to school. She was in love with a really cute boy in our grade and had been desperate to see him again. I'd pretended to join in her enthusiasm and had insisted that she keep me informed of any updates. But that really was the last thing I wanted to hear about. Being aware of how happy everyone else was just seemed to add to my misery.

Punching my fist into the cushion I'd been gripping tightly in my lap, I hurled it angrily at the coffee table in front of me then watched as it knocked one of my mother's favorite ornaments onto the floor, only to break in two.

"That's all I need," I thought to myself, sighing with self-pity, as I stood to pick up the remnants and tried to piece them together.

"I know! I'll ask dad to glue it." My dad was the master repair person when it came to gluing broken toys and objects around the house, but the solution was quickly whisked away when I remembered that he would not be coming home that evening.

And as if to add further to my misery, I watched my mother escort Barry to the front door, thanking him profusely for the work he had done. As they exchanged goodbyes, I caught him quickly glance in my direction.

"Did I imagine that?" I thought with disgust, "or did he actually just wink at me?" Instantly, the uneasy feeling in the pit of my stomach returned, as I realized how creepy that was.

Then with an abrupt jolt, I was hit with the premonition that something very dark and foreboding lay ahead.

Embarrassment…

Reluctantly, I forced myself to face another day at school. My brother had beaten me to the bathroom that morning and in typical Matt fashion, he'd left the floor flooded with water and his wet towel draped over the edge of the tub. The room reeked of his aftershave and I turned on the exhaust fan in the hope of clearing not only the excess steam away, but the disgraceful smell of the cologne he wore each day.

"The girls love it!" he'd said with a grin when I had commented on the scent that was later wafting around the breakfast table.

I watched in fascination as he devoured his second overfull bowl of cereal; as usual, the milk spilling onto the table top each time he dipped his spoon into the depths of the concoction in front of him.

"Gross!" I'd thought to myself, in disgust, shaking my head in disbelief that what he was saying could actually be true and at the same time wondering how he could possibly eat so much.

Deep down though and while I would never confess this, I secretly felt that he was pretty cool. My friends were always going on about how good looking he was and I would roll my eyes, pretending otherwise, all the while, feeling proud that he was my brother. I'd watch him and his group of friends from afar, while I sat with my own friends in our usual lunch spot at our old school.

Sometimes, I would have to go and talk to him and pass on a message from Mom or one of the teachers and I remembered the embarrassment I'd feel as I had to cross the grassy area in full view of all the other seniors.

His friends would always make comments and direct them my way.

"Hi, Julia!"

"How's it going, Julia?"

"I like your hair today, Julia!"

Matt would simply laugh and I could feel my face flush the way it always did when the focus of all those boys was directed towards me. I hated the way my embarrassment showed, but was completely helpless to prevent it.

I think it was probably because they were all older than me and actually quite a cool group. Some of them were really good looking as well and this just made the whole scenario that much more intense.

Although I continued to feel embarrassed, sometimes I'd make an excuse to visit Matt during breaks, knowing that I secretly enjoyed the attention I was receiving.

I remembered one time after cooking class, I'd taken some warm, freshly baked cupcakes over to his group so that he could share them with his friends. They all surrounded me and within seconds, the full platter I was holding had been emptied. The pride I had felt at their excited reaction, was one I still remember, and even Matt had been impressed, proud that it was actually his sister who had provided the unexpected treat.

After that episode, I seemed to constantly be attracting the attention of one particular member of his group.

"Any more cupcakes, Julia?" he'd ask with a cheeky grin.

"When are you cooking more cupcakes, Julia?"

The comments continued to flow and I thrived on the obvious interest that was coming from such a cool senior student. He even started calling me cupcake as a nickname and I would laugh with embarrassment, all the while, discreetly adoring all the fuss.

"I think he likes you," my friend, Cassie had remarked one afternoon and even though I'd brushed it off, I had hoped that it might actually be true.

Visions of those memories floated through my mind as I sat alone at the back of the bus heading to school. I'd tried to convince myself to stop focusing on what I'd left behind and to simply concentrate on the present moment. This was my life now and I would just have to accept it. I'd come to that realization the night before, while I lay in bed staring out the window deep in thought. And as those thoughts crossed my mind once more, I forced myself to focus on the new life I had just so recently embarked upon.

When the bus pulled to a stop at the front gate, I sighed with relief at the sight of some friendly faces who had also just arrived. With a determined attitude, I approached the group of girls who I now called my friends and we made our way to our first class of the day.

The morning passed by smoothly. That was until it was time for Math, where to my consternation, I found that Blake and Sara were also in my class and once again seated in the back row. The biggest challenge however, was the fact that by the time I'd found my way to the classroom, only one seat remained and that happened to be right in front of Sara.

"At least it's not beside her," I thought to myself, as I entered the room and sat down, all the while keeping my head bowed so I could avoid making eye contact with either of them.

It was when I looked towards the teacher that I was faced with another completely unexpected sight. Mr. Jamison, who apparently was the head of the Math department, was standing at the front of the class but he was not alone. By his side, stood a young guy dressed in chinos and a fairly tight fitting collared sports shirt that accentuated the fit looking body hidden underneath. He couldn't have been more than about eighteen or nineteen years of age. Every girl in the class was totally focused on him. Even the boys eyed him with interest. He looked pretty cool and it was obvious they were wondering who he was, as were the girls. But it was the girls who displayed the most dramatic reaction and I could feel their eyes riveted to the front.

He was extremely good looking and the girls around me began whispering and giggling to each other. As we listened intently, Mr. Jamison explained that this person, who was named Mr. Ryland and was obviously only a few years older than us, would be our Math teacher for the remainder of the semester. The original teacher had apparently taken leave due to an illness and Mr. Ryland had been assigned to replace him.

Immediately the class was abuzz with excited chatter, mainly from the girls, while the boys looked on with continuing interest.

"How old are you?" giggled one girl who sat at the front. "You don't look old enough to be a teacher!"

We all listened intently to his response. "I'm actually twenty-two," he explained. "I graduated from university six months ago and I've been a substitute teacher since then. But I'm very happy to now be a permanent teacher here."

"We're very happy too!" laughed a girl named Jackie.

Instantly the class cracked up and loud laughter filled the room. It was like an open invitation and it seemed that suddenly everyone was calling out their own opinions and comments.

"Do we call you sir or Mr. Ryland?" yelled Jackie from her spot near the back. She'd obviously been encouraged by the response from the rest of the class and gave the impression that she was ready to wreak havoc with the good looking, young teacher, who stood looking very uncomfortable at the front of the room.

I hadn't actually met Jackie before but I'd noticed her earlier in the day and that was probably because she appeared to be wearing the shortest skirt of anyone in the entire school.

Just as she opened her mouth to call out once more, Mr. Jamison's booming voice silenced the uproar and brought everyone to attention. "This noise level is totally unacceptable and if anyone chooses to continue with this sort of behavior, you'll be given after-school detention!"

The threat of detention was all that was needed to silence the group but the minute that he departed the room, the excited chatter, although definitely more subdued, quickly resumed.

While our new teacher managed to regain some semblance of order, the class certainly wasn't as quiet or as focused as they'd been when Mr. Jamison had been amongst us and it took Mr. Ryland quite some time to encourage everyone to actually pay attention to the work on the board.

I could see that most of the girls were having a hard time concentrating, and I had to admit, I was one of them. While I did manage to complete some work, I couldn't help but continually glance in the direction of the handsome young man in front of me. I was having trouble accepting him as our teacher! Maybe things were looking up after all. I mean if I had to go to Math class, having a teacher that looked like him, certainly made it so much more enjoyable!

Obviously though, I hadn't been discreet enough. With a jerk, I felt my chair being shoved roughly forward and it made a loud scraping sound on the worn floorboards. As soon as I turned around to see what had caused it, I instantly regretted my actions.

With an intense and unfriendly stare, Sara smirked, "Can't keep your eyes off him, Julia?"

The laughter from everyone within earshot just added to my humiliation and I felt my face flush, the familiar burning sensation creeping rapidly over my skin.

Mr. Ryland looked to the back of the room. "What's going on up there?" he queried.

"Oh nothing, sir," Sara replied in that sweet voice of hers that I remembered all too well. "It's just that Julia seems to be having a hard time concentrating today!"

The laughter that erupted rang in my ears and I sat there appalled.

"This can't be happening! It just can't!" the thoughts raced through my mind as I put my head down trying to avoid any more attention.

"You guys get on with your work!" Mr. Ryland's voice sounded over the noise. But then thankfully, the bell rang to signal the end of the lesson.

I quickly stood and made my way to the door, eager to escape, but I was stopped short by a strange sensation. It was that feeling one gets, knowing that someone else is staring. Sharply, I looked back, only to realize that Blake's eyes were focused intently on my own, almost as though he were seeing into the depths of my soul.

I held his gaze for just a moment. But then, recognizing that it was pitiful sympathy in his eyes and nothing more, I hurried out the door. His glance had only succeeded in humiliating me further and I fought my way through the throng of students to the safety of the lunch area, where I could hide amongst my friends and feel invisible.

Reaching the group, I sat down and tried to put the humiliation of the Math class and Blake's sympathetic stare out of my mind. As I listened in on the conversation and attempted to show an interest in what was being said, we were abruptly interrupted by the loudest and most outgoing member of the group, a girl named Lisa.

"Who is *that*?" she asked excitedly, in a voice that sounded like a freight train and could probably be heard right across that entire area of the school.

It seemed that everyone, including the groups of students who were sitting a distance away, abruptly turned in the direction she was pointing. To my horror, I could see that Mr. Ryland was on lunch break supervision duty and was obviously right in her line of vision. He was the one she had noticed and if others around us had not previously known he existed, they certainly did then.

"He's the new Math teacher." I mumbled quietly, trying to keep my voice down and avoid the stares that I could feel coming from almost every direction.

"OMG!" was Lisa's reply. "He's hot!!!!"

"I know," I said back to her. "That's the problem!"

Dad, where are you?

Rolling over in bed once more, I stared out the window. There was no moon but I could just make out the dull shine of one lone star in the far away night sky.

"That star resembles me," I thought. One lonely star desperately trying to find her place, but feeling completely isolated. Alone in a universe that is busily humming along each day with no thought for the lost soul who has no one to turn to and nowhere to go.

Tossing and turning once more, I recalled the day's events. The humiliation I had felt during Math filled me again with the burning shame that was becoming all too familiar. I simply could not believe that my past history and experiences with Sara were being repeated. Memories of the tortured nights where I had laid in the same bed and stared out the same window, haunted by the same mean girl at school who was making my life miserable; the recollection was way too intense to be forgotten.

Was this karma? Had I done something in a past life so that I was to be forever doomed to this life of misery, repeated over and over and over?

Stop feeling sorry for yourself, Sara!!

I have no idea where the abrupt reprimand came from, but there it was, clear and simple.

In the past, I had managed to survive and even conquer the demons in my life. Surely I was capable of doing it again!

To be a victim was a choice. I knew that was the case. If only I could once again become that strong, confident person I had been in middle school.

But so much had happened since then. And slipping back into self-pity mode, I thought about the support I once had; a best friend who I could always rely on, a boyfriend whom I adored and with whom I could share my heart and soul and a mother who actually cared about my well-being. These days she barely seemed to acknowledge my existence. She was there in body, but certainly not in spirit. Not for me, anyway!

Visions of Mom at the dinner table earlier that evening made me want to throw up! Who was that person? She seemed like a complete stranger to me!

I recalled glancing across the table at my brother, Matt, who seemed oblivious to what was actually going on in Mom's head. He was too concerned with his own life to be worrying about his mother and sister. It was his final senior year at school but that wasn't what was concerning him most. There were parties galore and too many good looking girls to consume his thoughts these days, so school work had been moved to the bottom of his priority list. He made it quite clear that moving back to our home in Carindale was the best thing that could ever have happened. His focus was on the prettiest girl in his grade at school and she was all that mattered.

"I'm going to ask her out!" he'd announced confidently to no one in particular as he excused himself from the table.

I had frowned at him and asked what on earth he was talking about.

"Do you think she'll say yes, Julia?" came his dreamy response.

"Yes, of course she'll say yes!" His own answer seemed to satisfy him and he had wandered off upstairs to the privacy of his room under the pretence of having homework to do.

41

But I knew that very little schoolwork would get done. Between Facebook, Instagram and all the other social media sites he regularly frequented along with the stupid games he still played on the computer, there would barely be time for homework!

Mom had fought a losing battle there. She'd tried to control Matt's computer use but soon found that defeat was inevitable. In the end, she had simply given up.

I was a completely different scenario. Where she had failed with her son, she seemed determined that her daughter was going to be her success story.

However, this ideal seemed to have gone by the wayside. Dramatically! I now appeared to be her last concern. In the past forty-eight hours, she'd become foreign to me. I mean, she still looked exactly the same, but she was definitely not the same person.

It was during dinner that she decided to share the events of her day. I was shocked to hear that Barry had been back. "There's so much work to be done around here and he's such a good tradesman. By the time your father gets home, the house will be looking as good as new!"

I had just stared at her, trying to figure out what was really going on in her head.

"He's so funny, Julia! Such a funny man!" Her fond recollection of this stranger was making me ill and I suddenly lost my appetite.

Then, as an afterthought at the end of dinner and as if abruptly remembering that she actually had a daughter who was experiencing the worst trauma of her life at this point in time, she asked, "Oh by the way, how was school today?"

"Fine," I replied, as I stood to clear the table.

"That's great, Julia! I knew that you'd settle in quickly!"

And that had been the end of the conversation.

Problem solved. Daughter okay. Son in room, doing homework. All the boxes ticked. Now I can focus on myself. And Barry!

I knew beyond any doubt that was how her mind was working. It was like she was suddenly facing some mid-life crisis or something and literally overnight, her needs had to be met, at all costs; even if that meant alienating her family.

"Daddy where are you?" A vision of my father floated into my thoughts. He had called earlier and told me that his week away had to be extended. It could possibly become two or even three weeks before he returned. But Mom didn't seem to mind. In fact, she appeared to welcome the idea.

As I lay there, thinking wistfully of my father and wishing he was here, I was abruptly transported back in time and became the little girl who once sat on his lap while he read a bedtime story. That had been my favorite part of the day during my childhood, but it now seemed like an eternity ago.

"You're such a daddy's girl!" Mom's words came back, haunting me now.

I rolled into my pillow, desperately trying to muffle the sobs that I was unable to prevent.

"Dad, please come home!"

Fear...

Hanging out with friends at the local shopping center after dark was a whole new experience for me. I'd never had the opportunity when we lived in the country because there were no large shopping complexes nearby. We had to go to the nearest city for that but I was too busy with my horses anyway.

However, it seemed that on Thursday evenings in Carindale, when the shops offered the luxury of late trading hours, this was what everyone did. At first I thought my mom would probably say no to the idea. In the past, schoolwork always came before anything else, especially on a week night, but she must have been way too preoccupied because to my complete surprise, she didn't even hesitate when I asked for permission.

I'd arranged to meet Lisa and some of the others from our group but it turned out that actual shopping was the last thing on their minds.

"We just come here to hang out and meet up with everyone," Lisa shook her head and frowned when I suggested that we scan through the sale items I had noticed hanging in a nearby store window. And as I looked around I could see various familiar faces, all sitting or standing in groups.

"It's a good place to check out the guys!" giggled Lisa as she sat eyeing off a tall, muscular looking boy probably two years older than her. It appeared that for high schoolers in Carindale, this was the whole aim of 'late night shopping.'

"See that guy over there?" she pointed out the one I had noticed her staring at. "He's a senior at Wesley High. And he's soooo cute!" It seemed she could not take her eyes off him.

"I met him at a party a month or so ago and we kind of hooked up, but I haven't seen him since. I'm going to go and say hello." Then without giving the idea another thought, she was gone.

I watched her as she walked away, looking completely confident and self-assured. "Wow!" I said to Beth, a girl who I had only met just that week. "She's keen! I'd never just walk up to a guy like that, especially a senior I hardly know."

"Well they did hook up at a party, remember!" Beth laughed.

The girls are so different here. The thought came abruptly to mind as I stood there feeling slightly uncomfortable about the scenario around me. Although, I had to admit I'd lived a pretty sheltered life on our farm, and what had occupied my time most was my pony, Bella. Horses were my obsession and most of my friends had felt the same way. We kind of had no time for boys. It just seemed that there were more important things to think about.

My thoughts then drifted to the scene I'd witnessed during lunch break at school the day before. I had stared mesmerized as Jackie, the outspoken girl from my Math class, joined her group of friends in stalking Mr. Ryland while he supervised the students in the lunch area. The blatant flirting of the girls was something I had never seen in action before, not in real life anyway.

Jackie in particular, had definitely been the most up front of them all. I remembered the flick of her blonde hair, heavily bleached and straightened which seemed to be the most popular style, as she laughed in unison with him over a joke they had obviously shared. She appeared so comfortable with the situation, as if it were a common occurrence to spend lunch break hanging out with the good looking, young Math teacher.

"That's so typical of Jackie." A girl in our group named Suzy rolled her eyes in disgust. "She'll probably try to get him to ask her out!"

"Or maybe she's hoping for an A in Math," laughed Lisa, who was also taking an avid interest in watching the scene in front of us unfold.

"This is better than a daytime soap opera!" she had continued jokingly. "At least we're being entertained during our lunch break!"

I had to agree with Lisa. It was certainly a scene I'd never witnessed before.

Beth's voice abruptly interrupted my thoughts, shaking me back to awareness of the shopping center scenario that I had found myself a part of. "Julia, didn't you used to go out with Blake Jansen? Some of the girls were talking about that today." Her unexpected question caught me completely off guard.

"Yeah, I did," I replied hesitatingly, not sure what they all knew about Blake and I. "But that was a long time ago when we were in middle school. Things have changed so much since then."

"Can you believe it? There he is now!" she grinned and nodded towards a cluster of bench seats that were situated in the center of the complex. The group had their backs towards us, but when one of the boys turned slightly, his profile came into full view and I recognized Blake immediately.

"I bet you wish you were still going out with him!" Beth continued. "He's so good looking!"

I ignored her comment and looked away, not wanting to think about Blake or Sara for that matter. But Beth wouldn't let the topic drop.

"So many girls wanted to go out with him, but he just didn't seem interested in anyone. And then Sara arrived. That's when it all changed. Although I'm not surprised! The two best looking people in the grade should be together. It's the way it usually works, don't you think?"

I could tell there was a tinge of jealousy in her tone. She was obviously envious of the Sara-Blake situation, and it made me curious to know how many other girls also felt the same way. But then she looked at me and must have realized that considering I was his ex-girlfriend, she should probably change the subject.

"Oh, sorry!' she mumbled apologetically. "I guess you'd rather talk about something else!"

"That's okay," I replied. "It was a long time ago that we were together. It's pretty much ancient history now."

And just as those words left my lips, I felt my skin tingle. It was a familiar sensation, one I had experienced before. But it was almost like *DÉJÀ VU*, and something made my head turn. It was a force, one that I could not resist. Then staring at me from a distance away, were the bluest eyes I knew I would ever see. Those eyes, how could I ever forget those eyes?

Then unexpectedly, I felt my stomach flutter and I gulped in recognition.

How could it be possible? After all this time I still had such strong feelings for Blake! I glanced once more in his direction, only to find him staring directly back at me.

That was when my insides went crazy; that weird and wonderful sensation when your stomach feels as though it's doing somersaults.

Instantly I turned away, a red flush creeping over my face. "Are you okay?" Beth asked worriedly. "You don't look very well."

"I...I'm alright," I stammered, desperately trying to regain control. "Actually on second thoughts, I do feel slightly nauseous. Maybe I'm coming down with something! I think I might call my mom to come and pick me up. I'll see you tomorrow Beth. Say goodbye to the others for me."

I looked in the direction of the girls we'd been standing with and noticed that they were now mingling with a group of boys whom I didn't recognize. Rushing off, I waved goodbye and left Beth to join them.

As I approached the exit I shook my head in dismay. "Julia, what is wrong with you! You're making a fool of yourself; stop being so ridiculous!"

Trying to regain some composure so my mom wouldn't give me the third degree on the phone, I called our home number, desperate to escape as quickly as possible. I wanted to go home, to the safety of my room where I could be alone and feel sorry for myself. The situation sucked and I knew I was making it worse. But I had no control. Feeling tears form in the corners of my eyes, I brushed them away and listened impatiently into the phone as I stood there waiting for someone to answer. But it just kept on ringing.

Trying again, I stood anxiously, hoping for someone to pick up. I knew that Mom was expecting me to be given a lift home but that didn't explain her absence. She hadn't mentioned that she was planning to go out. Although, in light of her erratic behavior over the past few days, anything was possible.

Irritably, I hung up and called her mobile. Waiting for what seemed like a ridiculously long time, I listened for the sound of the dial tone. Finally it connected, but went straight to message bank.

"That's just great!" I thought with a frustrated sigh as I considered leaving her a message. Mom was hopeless at answering her mobile, she never checked it. I decided that leaving a message was pointless.

Turning back towards the entrance of the center, I briefly pondered my options. The thought of re-joining the group and being confronted with Blake and Sara really did make me feel sick. So I rejected that idea immediately.

As I stood there, thinking of possible alternatives, I noticed a bus pulling away from the kerb and raced over to check the timetable that was attached to the wall of the bus shelter. I realized the last bus that would go in the direction of my house had already left.

Overcome with frustration, I gritted my teeth and headed off down the road, all the while muttering to myself irritably. "Where on earth are you Mom? Why aren't you answering your phone?"

I could just imagine her reaction if she knew that I was walking home when I was supposed to be getting a lift. But I didn't care! It was her fault for not answering when I called. What was the point in having a mobile if you weren't going to answer it, anyway?

Taking long, angry strides, I made my way along the thoroughfare, heading in the direction of my house; the light of the street lamps casting a dull glow on the concrete pavement in front of me. With a sigh, I reflected on my life at that point. Right then, I felt at a total loss, my once positive outlook that I had always strived to maintain, had appeared to have fallen completely by the wayside.

I had always believed that with a positive mindset, I could create my own reality, but since moving back to Carindale, my life seemed to be following a fast moving downward spiral. And I felt powerless to reverse it. But I just wanted my old life back! Why did things have to change so drastically? Surely I didn't deserve this!

As I continued along the street, I heard the faint sound of footsteps behind me, and gradually, the click, click, click became much louder and more distinct. Realizing that someone else was also heading in the same direction, I quickened my pace, hoping to increase the distance between us. Concentrating, I listened intently, all the while trying not to give in to the feeling of panic that was taking a firm hold in the pit of my stomach.

Surely, it was simply a case of my overactive imagination wreaking havoc with my senses. This often happened whenever I was nervous or excited and this particular occasion was no different. With my heart hammering in my chest, I tried to convince myself that I was being a drama queen and that the person behind me would innocently pass by, on their way home from a night out; possibly a late-night shopper who had been at the same complex I had left behind. But when the footsteps sounded only inches away, I became numb with fear.

"It's not safe to walk home alone at night time, Julia!" I heard my mother's voice ring in my ears. "Always make sure you're with a friend, or call me to pick you up. I don't want you walking alone at night!"

Her futile warning raced through my mind, just as I felt the brush of an arm against mine and my sharp intake of breath left me unable to utter a sound.

Frozen with fear, I stood rooted to the spot as I opened my mouth in an attempt to scream. But to my complete and utter relief, the man, a total stranger it seemed, raced past me and kept on going.

I gripped a hand to my chest, trying to ease the panicked rush of adrenalin that had left me breathless and in shock, and I forced myself to keep on walking. Breathing deeply I took in gulps of air, calming myself as I hurried along, at that point keener than ever to reach the safety of my house. Then, just as I turned a corner and the familiar outline of our neighbor's distinct two storey A-framed home appeared in view, I caught a glimpse of some movement from a section of tall, bushy shrubs that had been planted alongside the edge of the pavement. It created a thick screen of privacy for the vacant block behind it. That particular section of the street was poorly lit and I had to peer into the darkness to make out the dark shape that was partly hidden from sight.

When I realized abruptly that the movement wasn't being caused by an animal, I was instantly overcome with anxiety and fear. Then, as I approached that section of bush, peering out from his hiding spot, I could just make out the man who had only minutes earlier hurried past me. For a split second, I looked towards him in confusion; then, with a sudden flash of comprehension, realization hit.

It was at that instant, my feet seemed to take on a life of their own and sprinting, I raced for my front gate which stood at least fifty yards away, a silent sentinel in the darkness of the night. The scream I could hear seemed to be coming from someone else but when I felt his firm grip on my arm, the sound springing from my lips intensified and would not stop.

That vacant block had been there for years, and I remembered vaguely that my brother and I often used to play there in our childhood. It had been a meeting place for all the neighborhood kids and we had passed many hours playing hide and seek amongst those very bushes, the thick foliage creating a perfect place to hide. I remembered the tension I would feel when someone was close to finding me and I would hold my breath in the hope that I could remain hidden.

It was very strange how thoughts like those could flash by during moments of terror. The scene had a surreal quality and I felt as though I were a spectator, watching the events take place from above. But then, quite suddenly, I felt the grip on my arm loosen and I was able to break free. Perhaps it had been my piercing screams that had allowed me to escape, that and also the bright light that had appeared in the front window of the house across the road.

Without stopping or even once looking back, I fled to my front gate and down the darkened driveway. Racing up the steps to the front veranda, I fumbled for the key that we always kept hidden in the basket of one particular pot plant that hung overhead. My shaking fingers reaching inside, I felt around desperately for the familiar metal shape, realizing with a rising panic that it was nowhere to be found.

Frantically, I banged on the door and turned the knob, furiously pulling at it in every direction. My hope was that perhaps by some miracle it may actually be unlocked. But it would not budge. Then, as if in answer to my prayer, it abruptly swung open and I fell into the arms of my brother, Matt.

"What's your problem, Julia? It's a wonder you didn't break the door down!" His smart tone, dripping with attitude, just made me angry. My fear abating as I realized that I was safe at last, turned my anger to rage.

"Where have you been? Why didn't you answer the phone," I yelled. "Where's Mom? I needed a lift home and no one would answer the phone."

"Geez, Louise!" he said sarcastically, "what's got into you?"

"Some weirdo just tried to grab me! But do you even care? No, of course you don't. All you care about is yourself! I hate you!"

Screaming at him, my face flushed with tears and an overwhelming anger, I ran past him and up the stairs, slamming shut my bedroom door. Then I threw myself onto my bed and sobbed.

Decisions...

I woke to the sound of my alarm buzzing furiously in my ear. *Beeeep. Beeeep. Beeeeep. Beeeeep.*

"Shut that thing off!" I could hear my brother's voice from down the hallway.

It was so typical of him to be totally inconsiderate of anyone else in the house who might still be sleeping, but I guessed that my alarm would have already woken everyone up, anyway.

It was then my thoughts drifted to the night before and in a flash it all came flooding back. Rolling my head into the pillow, I squeezed my eyes closed, wanting to shut out the world and the day ahead. Just as I was considering the idea of faking an illness and taking the day off school, I heard my mother's voice.

"Time to get up you two! Barry will be here soon, he still has several days' work before he'll be finished doing all the jobs that need to be done. He's starting on the bathroom this morning, so if you want a shower, you'd better be quick!"

"Oh great!!" The loud groan that escaped my lips as I forced myself out of bed was full of disgust.

The option of going to school appealed much more than having to be in the house all day with Barry. He made me really uncomfortable. And I did not fancy a day at home with him hanging around. So with a sigh, I made my way quickly to the bathroom and locked the door before Matt could try to claim it first.

At breakfast, my mother's smiling, cheery mood just made me more irritable and for some reason I couldn't bring myself to even mention what had happened the night before. Although I couldn't resist complaining about the fact that she hadn't answered her phone.

"Oh sorry, darling!" she smiled at me, really quite unperturbed at the thought of missing my call. "I went out for a bit and must have accidentally switched my phone off."

I eyed her suspiciously then, wondering where she had actually been. It was so out of character for her to be acting this way. But wanting to be out of the house before Barry arrived, I didn't bother to question her further and grabbed an apple from the fruit bowl as I headed for the door.

"Have a great day," she called, as I closed the front door firmly behind me and made my way down our driveway towards the bus stop.

"Yeah, right!" I sighed. "And as if you really care!"

Miserably, I stood waiting for the bus, angry thoughts of my mother and her weird behavior playing on mind. But this was soon overcome with a sharp sensation of anxiety when, glancing around me, I happened to look in the direction of the vacant block down the street.

The fear I had felt just the night before, returned with a sharp jolt as I recalled the traumatic series of events. I knew that I really should report the incident, but what good would it do? I didn't have a clear description, so how could anything be done about it? But the memory made me very uneasy, and although it was full daylight and the street was busy with commuters driving to work, I could not help but constantly glance over my shoulder.

When I made my way into Math class later that morning, I rolled my eyes at the sight of Jackie and her entourage drooling over Mr. Ryland who had his back turned and was busily writing on the board.

"Check out that butt!" whispered Jackie to the girl alongside her. And giggling, they continued to drivel over the sight of the handsome young teacher standing in front of us.

Turning around with a frown, Mr. Ryland ignored the looks from the girls and asked everyone to open their books. He appeared to be a pretty good Math teacher and seemed to be capable of explaining tricky concepts in a way that was easy to understand. Definitely not like other Math teachers who I had experienced in the past, usually droning on with complex language and explanations that were completely beyond me. So much so that I had sat there unable to comprehend what they were talking about. Plus they'd been so boring and just seemed to talk on and on and on.

The Math teacher at my last school was so mind-numbing that one boy had actually fallen asleep at his desk. His friend had given him a quick poke but the boy had been out cold and it had taken quite a decent shake of his shoulders to actually wake him up. The look of confusion on his face when he scanned the room, realizing that everyone in the class was staring at him and in fits of laughter just exacerbated the situation, and the whole class had completely erupted. Even our teacher had started laughing and that was something we'd thought he was actually incapable of.

As I sat quietly in my seat listening to the sound

of Mr Ryland's mesmerizing voice, I forced myself to concentrate on the calculation that he was demonstrating on the board. While I acknowledged the fact that he was certainly very cute, I still thought of him as my Math teacher and had decided that his clear explanations would help me to improve my grades. As long as I managed to focus on what he was teaching! So, while I attempted to ignore the undercurrent of flirting that was taking place around me, I also ensured that at all costs I avoided eye contact with Blake, who sat in his usual spot next to Sara at the back of the room.

Sara had definitely noticed Blake glancing my way on a few occasions. I just wished he'd stop that. It made me uncomfortable plus the scathing expression that had appeared on Sara's face at one point, had been one that I remembered from many years earlier. I knew what she was capable of and I certainly didn't want to be antagonizing her in any way.

Blake was hers and she could have him. For all I was concerned, they deserved each other! I just wanted to be left alone!

Pushing all thoughts of Blake and Sara from my mind, I focused on the lesson and felt quite proud that I was able to do the work fairly easily. Jackie, I noticed, was having difficulty, although I was quite sure it was just an attempt to gain Mr. Ryland's attention. When he leaned towards her to point to an error she had made in her book, the manner in which she eyed him up and down, all the while twisting a lock of her blonde hair loosely around her index finger, made me want to throw up. It was clearly obvious that she thoroughly enjoyed having him so close. And I was convinced she was too busy checking him out, to concentrate on anything that he was saying.

Rolling my eyes, I gave a discreet shake of my head and looked back towards the work on the board. She was unbelievable. I just wondered how Mr. Ryland felt about it all. He'd have to be as blind as a bat, not to be aware of what was going on.

"He's probably used to it!" Lisa had said, when I described Jackie's behavior during our lunch break later that day. "He's so good looking, I'm sure it happens to him all the time. Especially when there's girls like Jackie in his class. She just can't help herself!"

I was about to comment further on the openly inappropriate behavior that I was struggling to come to terms with, when the conversation was abruptly interrupted by Suzy, who had just received a notification on her phone about a party on the weekend. Apparently everyone in the group had been added to the event and the news quickly took priority over everything else they'd been talking about

"Chloe Henderson throws the best parties!" Beth exclaimed. And looking towards me she continued excitedly, "You have to come, Julia!"

"Yes, Julia. You'll love it!" Lisa chimed in. "I'll ask her to add you to the event."

They all seemed very insistent that I should go and I felt pleased to be included.

"I don't have a Facebook account, so I have no idea of any of the details," I replied, reminding her of the fact that she had been bewildered by when I'd mentioned it earlier in the week.

"What? Your mom won't let you on Facebook? That really sucks!" Lisa's response had been evidence of her disbelief that someone our age did not use Facebook, or any other type of social media.

"I simply could not live without Facebook and Instagram!!" she had blatantly declared. It appeared that to Lisa, this was a life or death situation and I began to understand what a freak I must seem in her eyes, not to mention the others in our group.

They were all really nice to me, even though I was so different to them. They obviously thought I was a bit strange at times and this was made clear by their odd looks at various things I said or did. But good heartedly, they usually just laughed and shook their heads.

"You're so naïve and innocent, Julia!" Lisa had said just that morning. "But don't worry, you'll soon learn. By hanging out with us it won't take you long!" And with a toss of her long brown hair, she had taken off to join a group of boys sitting nearby, one of whom she had a huge crush on.

I really did just want to belong. These girls had rapidly become my friends and I was grateful to be a part of such a fun group. Looking across the grassed area where we were sitting, I noticed a girl in our grade called Amy, sitting on her own, a book in her hands as usual and totally engrossed in what she was reading. The thought of being a loner like Amy, made me shudder. But she seemed quite content with her situation. The fact that she sat on her own most of the time, didn't seem to bother her at all. In a world of her own, filled with books and study, she appeared unaffected by what was going on around her.

Most people thought she was weird, but in a way, I envied her. She was not upset by the likes of Sara and Jackie and others like them. She didn't appear to have the deep-seated need to fit in. Although I didn't know what really went on in her head, on the surface she appeared to breeze through life. The usual teenage dramas that in reality were trivial and of no importance, didn't seem to worry her. She was far more interested in her world of books and knowledge.

But that could never be me. I needed to be a part of a group and I longed for a best friend, someone I could really talk to. Thoughts of the attack the night before flashed through my mind. That was the term I was using to describe it. Even though in theory, it was only an attempted attack, it was still an attack and I desperately wished for a really close friend with whom I could share the terror I'd felt.

When I'd last spoken to Cassie on the phone she'd been totally consumed with her new boyfriend. He was all she'd wanted to talk about and when she had finally decided to take an interest in what I'd been up to, he arrived at her house to take her out on a date. With a quick goodbye, she'd promised to call me back sometime soon, but I had a feeling it might be a while before I heard from her again.

Then I thought of Millie. The relationship we had once shared had been the kind that every girl needs. BFFs forever! I still had that photo sitting on a shelf in my room and I really looked forward to her return. I wondered hopefully, if we could ever resume our special friendship.

Abruptly and with a sudden determination, I looked around the group of girls surrounding me and decided that I would go to that party on the weekend. What else did I have to look forward to? A night at home with my mom? How boring would that be! Although she probably had other plans, perhaps even with Barry.

The mere thought of that creepy man who right at that moment was in my house, made me very uneasy. I just hoped he was gone by the time I arrived home. Otherwise, I'd have to hide in my room until he left. There was something about him that I just did not like. Creepy. That was the only way I could describe the way he made me feel. And I was not at all comfortable with the interest my mother seemed to have in him.

I wished Dad was home. Then everything could become almost normal again.

Almost.

The party...

"I need Chloe's phone number." Mom was very insistent that she should have Chloe's number after I mentioned I was keen to go to her party on the weekend.

She had wanted to call Chloe's mom, but that was just so embarrassing. I'm not in middle school anymore. She treats me like a child. Seriously! She's such a control freak!

"If I have her number, then I'll feel more at ease. And by the way, pick up time will be at 10:30." She seemed adamant that there was going to be no compromise regarding the time.

"10:30? Seriously, Mom! The party will only just be starting then. Can't we make it 12?"

I could not predict my mother's responses anymore. She seemed to be all over the place. One day it was as though she hardly cared what I did and the next, she was back to her old controlling ways. But to be honest, I think I preferred it when she was preoccupied. At least then I could do pretty much what I wanted!

But my pleading look must have won her over because after a moment's hesitation, she relented. "Alright, 12:00. I'll be waiting out the front. Just make sure you're there!"

I was so glad that I'd been able to convince her to extend the curfew. 10:30 was way too early and my prediction had been correct. By 10:30, the party was only just getting under way.

When I first arrived, I'd felt pretty awkward. Getting a ride with Lisa had seemed a good idea at the time but as soon as she saw her friend, the senior from Wesley High, she left me to go and join him. I hadn't expected people from other schools to be there and there were a lot of unfamiliar faces, some of them definitely seniors.

Feeling totally awkward standing on my own in a corner, I decided to head for the bathroom. An attack of nerves had taken over plus I didn't want to be looking like a loser with no one to talk to. I hoped that if I killed some time, others from our group might arrive.

When I eventually returned to the party, there were a lot more people and I was very relieved to spot Beth, Suzy and some of the others. With a sigh of relief I walked over and joined them. Almost instantly I realized that there was definitely something peculiar going on.

"Juliaaa! It's so good to see you here!" Beth was drawling in an odd manner; I'd never seen her act or speak that way before. Then I noticed her gripping something in her hands, but in the darkened room I couldn't be sure what it was. Taking a closer look, I spotted a dark colored drink flask, but I suspected that it contained something much stronger than water or soda.

"Oh, do you want a drink? Here Julia, have a drink!" she giggled uncontrollably and this just set the others off. Within seconds, they were all in fits of laughter but I had no idea what they were actually laughing about.

"I'm ok!" I replied shyly, feeling uncomfortable and slightly on edge.

The only time I'd tried alcohol was at Christmas a couple of years earlier, when I drank several glasses of fruit punch, only to find out afterwards that it had been provided for the adults and was laced with some type of strong liqueur. My dad found me asleep on the couch later in the day, and when he woke me up I had a throbbing headache.

But the girls would not allow me to be the only one amongst them who wasn't drinking. "Come on," Beth insisted. "Just have a sip!"

Reluctantly, I took the bottle from her and lifted it to my lips, tentatively taking a small taste but without warning, it was brusquely titled upwards. Glancing sideways, I could see that Beth was literally pouring it down my throat. Gasping for breath, I looked towards her.

"A tiny sip won't do anything, Julia!" Laughing, she took the bottle from me, had one more swallow herself and then leant against the wall for support.

"Hey, there's some cute guys here!" indicated Suzy as she scanned the room. And just as she said that, Blake walked in. Following along closely behind him however, was Sara who had a firm grip of his hand.

Her air of confidence as she took in the scene around her was brimming with the self-assured manner that she was renowned for. Dressed in a gorgeous white skirt that showed off her amazing long legs, she caught the eye of every guy in the room. She had such a great figure and always looked so good. Her sequinned blue top was low cut and set off her blue eyes and complexion perfectly. And I looked on with envy at the cleavage she was flaunting. No wonder she had the attention of all the guys in the room! It was so unfair! Why was I still so flat chested? Without a padded bra, I'd look like I had absolutely nothing in that department, which was pretty much the case anyway.

"OMG!" breathed Suzy. "She is so up herself!!"

"I can't stand her," Beth said, full of contempt.

"Blake is such a nice guy, I seriously do not understand what he sees in her!"

"Have a look at that body!" exclaimed Abbie, who had just joined us. "What do you mean you don't know what Blake sees in her?"

Turning away in disgust, the girls searched for their flasks and continued drinking. All the while I discreetly took in the scene around me.

Blake and Sara had disappeared into the kitchen and I was glad that they were no longer nearby. Although, I could feel that I'd become pretty relaxed and wasn't even really bothered about them being there.

I spotted Lisa, sitting on a comfortable sofa in a corner along with her friend, the senior from Wesley High. The two of them were completely oblivious to the crowd of people around them, evidently way too focused on other things and it seemed they couldn't keep their hands off each other. There were several other couples who appeared to be similarly preoccupied but when the music was abruptly turned to what seemed like maximum volume, it was like a magnet attracting everyone's attention. Then one after another, people began to dance. Grabbing hold of Beth's bottle, I took another large gulp before joining her and the others on what had become the dance floor.

In my own little world, I moved to the sound of one of the latest hit songs. The party was raging and I felt totally at ease in the fun atmosphere surrounding me. I couldn't remember when I'd last felt so relaxed, and closing my eyes, I swayed my hips to the rhythm of the music.

Dancing had always been one of my all-time favorite things to do. That was until horse riding took over. I remembered vaguely, the dance competitions that Millie and I had entered and the prizes we'd won. Hip hop was my preferred style and at one point I'd been aiming for a national title, but then we'd moved to the country and dancing had gone by the wayside.

Everyone started singing and the noise level rose to a deafening roar. The party was certainly a happening event and as I looked around, I realized how much fun I could have if I just went with the flow and enjoyed myself.

Without warning, I felt a pair of large hands on my hips, moving my body to the rhythm of the song. However, music was in my soul and it felt completely natural to be dancing that way.

The hands belonged to someone behind me, I had no idea who, but I was so engrossed in the music and the atmosphere surrounding me, that I felt unaware; the scene was almost surreal. The caressing of my skin as fingertips began to explore under the lower edge of my fitted top, was like a rhythmic massage.

Tuning into my own little world while I danced and moved, completely carefree, created in me a sense of ease; a state I had not enjoyed for quite some time.

Creeping steadily up my torso, the hands continued to grope but when I felt the unwelcome sensation of heavy breathing in my ear and against my cheek, I was rapidly brought to a level of somewhat conscious awareness.

The invasion of my personal space was not his for the taking. I had not invited this person to grab hold of me and I was irritated and uncomfortable about his close proximity and familiarity with my body. The smell of alcohol on his breath began to turn my stomach and I felt nausea rise in my throat as I tried to push the unwanted hands away.

"Hey, what's up?" I could hear the slur of a strange voice in my ear.

I wanted to escape. I needed fresh air and I needed to get outside.

"Leave me alone!" I demanded.

But the rough hands were insistent, and he did not want to let go.

"Baby, just dance with me!"

"Get lost!!" I yelled in frustration and struggled once more to break free from his grasp.

Just then, I saw the hands of another boy. They came from nowhere and abruptly grabbed the shoulders of the guy harassing me. Roughly pulling the offender away, I heard Blake's voice over the din of the music.

"Hey, leave her alone!"

I stared at Blake then, in shock and disbelief that he had stepped in to help me. With a last glance towards him, the surprise and confusion evident on my face, I turned towards the front door and raced out into the darkness of the night. I needed to hide away; to find a space of my own.

Why was he in my life? Why did he still have such a strong effect on me? How could I ever get over him when he always seemed to be nearby?

The fresh air hit my face and my head started spinning from the alcohol. I slumped gratefully down on the stairs that led from the tiled veranda to the garden below. Leaning against the railing for support, I breathed in welcome gusts of fresh night air. I knew I hadn't had that much to drink but it had obviously found its way straight to my head and I wished that I'd taken my mother's advice when she suggested that I eat something before going out.

Lost in my thoughts and trying to control the spinning sensation I'd been overcome with, I was interrupted by the gentle touch of a hand on my shoulder. Whipping around ready to fend off the unwanted attention, I came face to face with Blake, his piercing blue eyes staring into my own.

"Is it ok if I sit here?' he asked quietly.

Without acknowledging him, I turned back and concentrated on the scene in front of me. I had to find something to focus on; anything but the person beside me at that moment in time.

Glancing around at my surroundings, I took in the beautiful garden at the foot of the stairs, neatly landscaped with a multitude of leafy plants and large flowering shrubs. If ever I had my own place, I would love to have a garden just like that. The thought flashed through my mind as I tried my hardest to pretend that I was alone.

He touched my arm then; ever so lightly. Just a simple gesture, innocent really. But the hidden meaning was so very clear.

Ignoring him, I looked in the opposite direction.

"Can we talk, Julia? I really need to talk to you."

I refused to answer. I could not respond. I simply did not trust myself to speak.

"Please, Julia?"

The pleading in his tone, forced me to turn my head, but instantly I wished I hadn't.

Those eyes, so blue and so familiar, staring intensely into mine; I was powerless to look away.

"I still love you, Julia!"

My gasp was involuntary, but full of shock and anguish at hearing the words I had so longed to hear. How could this be happening? Deep inside, I knew it was wrong. I stood, eager to escape his presence. I just couldn't be around him. I had to leave.

Racing through the garden towards the street, I frantically searched the darkness. I needed a place to go, somewhere to hide. But his hand, a sudden firm grip on my arm, stopped me from going further. And when I turned to look at him, the expression in his eyes, those penetrating blue eyes that I had once so desperately adored, forced me again to remain still; it was almost trance like, hypnotic, as if moving from that very spot was beyond my control.

Then, as if in a dream, his lips were on mine. And when he gripped me close, I shivered in response. The current passing through me was electric. And I knew that if I were to be struck by lightning right then, it would feel exactly the same way.

I lingered for a moment, just an irresistible moment to savor the wonderful sensation that was coursing through me, right through to my inner core.

Until realization hit. It was abrupt and intense but it jolted me instantly to my senses. This was wrong. This shouldn't be happening! I had to get away.

Breaking free, I raced to the darkened street, just as my mother's car pulled into the kerb.

Daring to risk a look behind me, I spotted Sara, standing at the top of the stairs. Her gaze followed mine as I glanced once more towards Blake and then hastily opened the car door so I could escape into its safe interior, away from her menacing stare.

Had she seen our embrace? Had she seen Blake kiss me? Shivering with apprehension, I forced myself to focus on the road ahead. "Do not look back, Julia. Whatever you do, do not look back!"

Switching off from my mother's incessant

chatter and curious questions about the party, from which we could hear music still blasting loudly as we drove away, I turned my head and looked out the car window into the blackness beyond.

As I stared at my reflection, the despair clear on my face, I thought of the scene I had just left behind.

And I was consumed with a sensation of dread.

Unexpected...

He kissed me again. It was ever so tender and then he pulled me close. I was powerless to resist. This time, I was not going to break away. The feel of his muscular body within my grasp sent shivers of delight right through to the innermost part of me. The part that forces ones' stomach to drop with the absolute thrill of it all. And as I felt his strong hands gently stroking the curve of my back, I was in heaven, and wished I could contain that very moment. A treasure to replay and enjoy until the end of eternity.

Then I opened my eyes. And within a flash, the dream was whisked away.

Desperately wanting to return to that blissful state, I closed my eyes once more. It had been such an incredible dream, so intense, so real. I wanted to recapture it, to go back to that magical moment. But it was no use. The dream was gone and I was forced to confront the scene around me. It did not include Blake and it certainly did not include his embrace.

It was a miserable day, gray and cold. Rain and wind lashed against my window as the unpruned tree branches noisily scraped the corrugated rooftop. Sighing with disgust, I lay there, staring into the dimness of the day outside. But eventually, I took comfort in the fact that at least it was Sunday and I did not have to go to school.

Reaching a hand to my lips, I recalled his kiss. Not the one from my dream, but the real kiss, the one he had given me just the previous night. My heart had melted at his touch and for a split second I had remained, my eyes closed, to enjoy the wonder of that moment. But then reality had crashed through my senses like a freight train, unstoppable and dangerous. And I'd had to escape.

He belonged to Sara now. And I was determined never to be a cheater by luring away the boyfriend or partner of another. I knew it happened regularly and the offenders, the ones at fault, usually didn't care. They had no regard for the feelings they would crush and the devastation their choice would cause.

I had once vowed that I would never be like them. And I knew that I could not live with myself if I broke that promise.

There was another factor though. And I acknowledged that I'd be lying if I didn't admit my pride had managed to get in the way. He'd chosen to be with her; the arch-enemy of my past. The one person who had made me so miserable for so long! Recollections of the tormented days and I nights I had suffered from Sara's abuse were still fresh in my mind and I could not let that go.

Anyone but her!!!

How could he ever have stooped so low?

Thoughts of Sara's evil stare the night before as I'd fled the scene, came quickly to mind. Had she seen us? Did she know?

I prayed for the answer to be no. But the sinking feeling in my stomach belied my suspicion that it could be otherwise.

Avoidance! That would have to be my tactic in future. Whenever I saw him, I would just have to walk the other way. Surely he will then understand that it's the way it has to be. And the only person he has to blame is himself!

As long as I don't show any interest, Sara should be fine. I tried to convince myself that it would all be okay.

But why was I still so miserable? Why did I still feel such a sense of loss?

Millie always used to say that the best way to get over someone was to replace them with someone else. Maybe that was the key?

I knew that it worked for my brother. I thought about his last girlfriend, who had dumped him unexpectedly. Matt had been devastated. I'd never seen him that heartbroken and I had felt so sorry for him. I never thought he'd get over it.

And then, less than a week later, he'd come home beaming.

"Why are you so happy?" I remember asking him.

"Oh, there's this really hot girl at school!" he explained. "I can't understand why I've never really noticed her before! I think I'll ask her out!"

I actually stared at him, in total disbelief.

"What???" he asked. "What's the problem?"

I simply rolled my eyes and shook my head. Words could not describe right then, my inability to fathom how boys' minds worked. And I still didn't think that I could mimic his behaviour. It just wasn't possible.

Just then, the smell of breakfast cooking wafted under my door and interrupted my thoughts. Abruptly, visions of my brother and his fickle attitude disappeared from my mind as I realized how hungry I was, especially after missing dinner the evening before. Food! Maybe that would help take my mind off my situation. And I hopped out of bed and padded down the carpeted stairs to the kitchen.

Sundays were traditionally Pancake Day for our family. Dad was the master chef in our household and his pancakes were to die for! I hadn't ever tasted any that were better than his. Thinking of him, I reminded myself to give him a call as soon as we'd finished eating. I missed him so much. He was the easy-going parent of the two and along with being a great cook, he also had a fantastic sense of humor. Even my friends laughed at his lame jokes. I think it was the manner in which he told them. People couldn't help but laugh. He could be such a funny man!

Striding into the kitchen, my stomach grumbling loudly, I was rapidly stopped short by the sight of the unwanted but familiar figure parked on a stool at our kitchen bench. His back was towards me, but the relaxed and comfortable manner in which he sat completely at ease in my mom's company while she cooked our breakfast, just made me angry.

Moments before, I'd been thinking of my dad and wondering what he was actually doing right at that very point in time. Then, totally unexpectedly, there he was, Mom's new *friend* sitting on Dad's favorite stool as she flipped pancakes on the stove.

I was still glaring, speechless, when Mom looked up, realizing that I was standing there. And that was when he turned around.

"Hi, Julia! How are you today?" I think the unfriendly stare that Barry was faced with forced him to explain. "I left some of my tools here the other day and because I was in the neighborhood this morning, I thought I'd drop in and grab them. But your Mom insisted that I stay for breakfast!"

I kind of grunted in response, ignoring the frown that Mom was directing towards me. But when I glanced again at

Barry, I instantly felt the expression on my face turn to one of revulsion. It seemed quite clear that his eyes were wandering over my bare legs but it was the manner in which he was doing this that filled me with the sick feeling of dread. At first I thought I must surely be mistaken, but when his eyes met mine, the sly grin which appeared on his face clearly betrayed his disgusting thoughts.

I was still in my pyjamas, a long-sleeved flannelette shirt and a pair of silky pink boxer shorts. They obviously weren't a matching set. I had just thrown them on before climbing gratefully into bed the night before. The shorts had been a present from Mom for my last birthday and were my favorites. But I did not feel at all comfortable with Barry's wandering eyes staring at me in that way and I tried to tuck my legs under the kitchen table so they were hidden from view.

If I hadn't been so ravenously hungry, I would have excused myself and gone without breakfast. But it wasn't only my appetite that kept me glued to my chair, it was the knowledge that a sudden exit would have also caused a scene.

"Julia, you're so rude! What has gotten into you?"

My mother's voice was clear in my head and I could imagine not only her words but her tone, and it just wasn't worth the consequences I would later have to suffer. So I gritted my teeth and silently ate the pancakes that she served onto a large plate. I gulped down what I could, desperate to finish eating so I could make my escape.

Even the sight of my brother when he finally made his way down the stairs, did nothing to calm my unease. It seemed that he was totally oblivious to what was going on around him and didn't hesitate to accept Barry's pitiful excuse for being in our house.

"Yeah, sure!" I'd thought to myself when he attempted once more to explain his presence in our kitchen. "You just conveniently happened to be in our neighborhood at that time on a Sunday morning."

That scene was foremost in my mind when I spoke to my dad on the phone later that day, but I was conscious not to mention the surprise visit. I also did not relay the fact that Mum had cooked us pancakes but we'd had to share them with the creepy tradesman who had seemed to become a familiar figure in our household. And neither did I mention how uncomfortable he made me feel.

All I did say to my dad was that I wanted him to come home.

"Next weekend, I'll be back. And how about we all go out for a nice dinner? You can choose the restaurant!" His cheery reply did little to lift my spirits.

"That'll be great Dad," I tried to sound enthusiastic, but was finding it very difficult. The sinking feeling in my stomach would not go away.

After a little more idle chatter I sadly hung up the phone. Then, one slow step at a time, I climbed the stairs to my room. I didn't know if the correct term was premonition or intuition, but whatever it was, I had a strong sense that things would never be the same again.

Guilt...

"Did you hear the news?"

Beth was beside herself when I arrived at school on Monday morning. It was quite clear there was something really exciting she was desperate to share and couldn't wait to include me in the latest gossip.

"What?" I asked, curiously. "What happened?"

As the words spilled from her mouth, I stood agape, watching as she spoke. She was talking so quickly and could not seem to stop. It was the weirdest sensation but I could not take my eyes from her mouth. Her cherry colored lip gloss glistened brightly as the light of the morning sun reflected off the nearby window. It was such a pretty color and I made a mental note to ask her what it was so that I might also be able to buy some for myself. Since moving back to Carindale I had started wearing make-up but I did not have any lip gloss that was as pretty as Beth's.

Weird! That was the only word I could think of to describe my thoughts right then. Beth had just shared the most staggering news and I was thinking about buying lip gloss. The mind certainly was an incredible thing; the ability to completely switch off like that and focus on something as bizarre as lip gloss. Was that a normal phenomenon? Or was I really starting to lose it? Her voice had become a background blur, an intense monologue that went on and on and on. I stood silently, all the while fascinated, as her sparkling lips continued to move.

It is crazy though, how one's thoughts can abruptly change. Because in the blink of an eye, the full extent of what she was saying finally filtered through to my conscious mind and I began to process the news that she was attempting to share.

Tentatively, I looked around me, wondering if others had heard and were also discussing this latest piece of hot gossip.

"Blake Jansen and Sara Hamilton have split up!"

With escalating alarm, I continued to process Beth's words. Even though she'd been speaking for what seemed like a very long time, it was really only those words that I fully grasped. Then, gulping anxiously, I dared to hope there may be the slightest chance this news may actually be untrue.

Oblivious to my reaction, she raced on, "Can you believe it? Everyone's in shock!" Beth seemed barely able to contain her excitement. It was as though this were the news of the century, the gossip that everyone would be desperate to hear.

"She was so keen to be his girlfriend in the beginning, you know. No one ever expected that this would happen! And do you know what! Apparently she saw him kissing some other girl at the party on Saturday night and when she confronted him, he dumped her! That's what Jackie heard. OMG! I can just imagine Sara's reaction. I'm sure she's never been dumped before! She would be absolutely furious!!"

Beth continued on and on. The feeling of dread was like lead in my stomach. But it appeared she had no idea that I was the one who Blake had kissed. Perhaps Sara didn't know either? I felt a sudden flicker of hope.

I knew beyond any doubt though, that if all of this were true and Blake did dump Sara because of me, she would not let it go. The humiliation would be too much. To be dumped would be bad enough, but for it to happen because of me, would be absolutely intolerable.

"Nooooo!" I screamed silently. "Why did I let him kiss me? How did I let that happen?" And walking the length of the hallway, Beth talking on and on and on, I just wanted to yell at her. "Stop, Beth!! Stop talking! I don't want to know!"

It was with sheer relief that I was finally able to enter my History class and leave Beth to continue on to her own classroom, situated further down the hall. I was convinced that I could not take her babbling for another second. It had taken every last reserve of self-control not to yell at her to shut up!

I just wanted to be left alone, to hide away at the back of the room in order to fully process the situation I had inadvertently created.

It was quite peculiar, such a contradiction! I was fully aware that my desire to be with Blake again had been intense. He was all I could think about and if I had been told, just a week earlier, that I would have the chance to be with him again, I would have been overcome with joy. But not this way. This was not how it was meant to happen!

As I sat down in my usual spot by the window, I smiled briefly at the girl next to me, trying desperately to appear as though nothing was wrong. But my mind was reeling. Reeling with the recognition that I had caused this sudden end to their relationship. I had done exactly what I'd sworn I would never do.

"If only I hadn't been drinking, I'm sure it would never have happened. Oh why did I have to go to that party in the first place?"

Frantically trying to ease the growing panic that was threatening to erupt inside me, I turned towards the open window and breathed in deeply, grateful for the intake of much-needed fresh air. When I noticed the curious look my teacher appeared to be directing my way, I forced myself to remain calm and pretended to focus on the work on the board, all the while striving to fight off visions of Sara, her evil stare boring into my soul. I knew that she was not in my history class, but I had the uncanny sensation that she was right there, a penetrating presence right by my side.

Sighing with relief at the sound of the bell which ended the lesson, I raced towards the bathroom where I splashed cold water over my face. Then made my way to the library, eternally grateful for the study period that I'd been assigned. I found a spare desk in a corner, where I could sit unnoticed and avoid the attention of other students. I did not want to face anyone and I certainly did not want to face Blake or Sara. I just wanted to hide away, hide away and be left alone.

It was at the end of the day, after the final bell had rung that I opened my locker to shove my books inside. I was desperate to get home. I'd been feeling unwell all day. Perhaps it was the food I'd purchased from the canteen during the lunch break. Even though I had barely eaten anything, I had noticed something strange about the flavored milk. It may have been sour, an old carton that was out of date and should have been cleared from the fridge. Maybe that was the cause of the nausea I was feeling.

But deep down I knew that was not the case. Sour milk wasn't to blame for the sick leaden sensation that had remained in my stomach all day. I'd been constantly on edge, worried I would come face to face with Sara in the hallway. I imagined the words she would scream at me while everyone stared.

"Julia Jones! You bitch! You just couldn't stand to see me with him, could you?"

The feeling of guilt coursed through me, it seemed to spread like wildfire. Although I hoped and prayed she wouldn't know I was to blame, I really didn't expect that possibility to eventuate.

There was another issue though. Regardless of the guilt I felt, the words I imagined being confronted with, the words I could picture Sara spitting forth like toxic venom, were actually true.

"You couldn't stand to see me with him, could you?"

Watching the two of them together had been unbearable. It was a sight I'd been unable to accept. Anyone but Sara Hamilton. Anyone but her!

I began to break into a heavy sweat. I could feel the beads of perspiration dripping from my forehead. Wiping my face on the back of my sleeve, I took a deep breath. My mind was woozy and I could not think straight.

"Why won't my locker open?" My frustration was worsened by the fact that I felt so unwell. I just wanted to put my books away and go home. And if I didn't hurry I was going to miss the bus.

I tried the combination one more time. "If I can't open it, I'll just have to take my books with me." The thought filtered vaguely through my mind as I fiddled with the clasp, in one last ditch attempt to open the lock.

When finally the door swung wide and I looked into the dark interior, I blinked. Perplexed, I reached inside to retrieve the strange shape that was staring out at me.

"Where on earth did this come from?" Muttering to myself, I stood confused and wary. It was the strangest looking thing I had ever seen.

In my vague and muddled state, my mind refused to process exactly what the unusual object was. But then, realization dawned. It was an instant comprehension, a sudden and total understanding of what was in my hand. Speechless, and riveted to the spot, all thoughts of the bus that I would surely miss if I did not hurry, disappeared from my mind.

Right then, missing the bus had become the very last of my concerns.

Overcome with a sudden flush of heat, I felt my head spin. Images of Sara flooded my senses. Even in my dazed and disoriented state, I could see her eyes, cold and menacing as they pierced through the fog of shock and nausea that was threatening to erupt all over the scene in front of me.

Gasping for breath, I turned cautiously, daring to look behind me, convinced she would be there smirking, mocking, laughing; triumphant in her revenge. But to my utter surprise, there was no menacing stare. In fact very few people remained in the hallway where I stood as I tried to comprehend the scenario I'd been faced with.

And then, I felt my eyes roll back into my head, just before everything went black.

***

Find out what eventuates next, in

Book 2

ROLLER COASTER LOVE

Available NOW!!

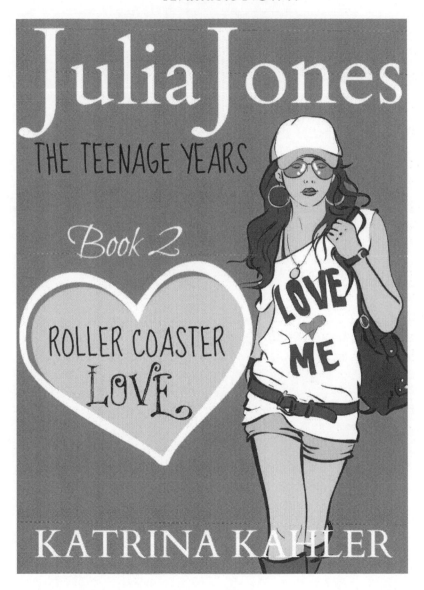

ANNOUNCING A NEW SERIES!!

This fabulous new series fills the gap after Julia was forced to move to the country with her family.

It continues the story of Julia Jones' Diary but has a whole new twist, one that all Julia Jones' Diary fans are sure to enjoy.

A new girl called Emmie unexpectedly arrives in Carindale and meets Millie. But Emmie has a secret, a secret that must remain hidden at all costs.

What happens to Julia, Blake, Sara and all the others and how does Emmie's sudden appearance impact Julia and her friends?

Find out now in

Mind Reader – Book 1: My New Life

OUT NOW!!

Read all about Julia's friend, Ella

in the exciting New Series…

Angel

Book 1

Guardian

AVAILABLE NOW!!

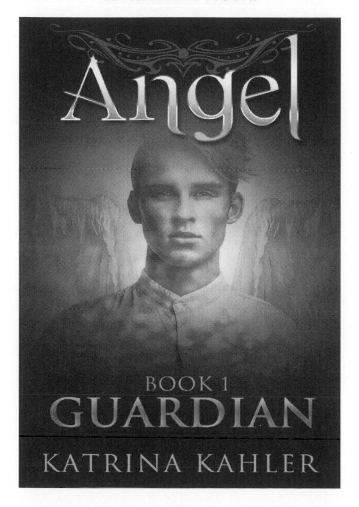

15984686R00049

Printed in Great Britain
by Amazon